ROLLO AND JULIET... FOREVER!

by Marjorie Weinman Sharmat
pictures by Marylin Hafner

Doubleday & Company, Inc., Garden City, New York

Library of Congress Cataloging in Publication Data

Sharmat, Marjorie Weinman.
  Rollo and Juliet, forever!

  SUMMARY: Rollo and Juliet's friendship is
temporarily interrupted by a quarrel.
  [1. Friendship—Fiction. 2. Quarreling—Fiction.
3. Cats—Fiction] I. Hafner, Marylin. II. Title.
PZ7.S5299Ro   [E]

Library of Congress Catalog Card Number 80-628
ISBN: 0-385-15784-3 Trade
ISBN: 0-385-15785-1 Hardbound

9 8 7 6 5 4 3 2

To friendship,
true-blue
and otherwise

Rollo Cat and Juliet Cat played tag together, jumped rope together, and always said pleasant things to each other.

"Have a very fine day full of blue skies and soft clouds, Rollo," said Juliet.

"And may your day sparkle with a good golden glow from the sun, Juliet," said Rollo.

Rollo and Juliet would sit for many hours on the big sofa in Rollo's house and talk quietly.

"Our friendship is true blue," Juliet would say. "Through sad times, good times, rain, sleet, crackling thunder and prickly heat, our friendship will go on."

"And on," said Rollo. "Forever."

"At least," said Juliet.

One day when Rollo was suppposed to go to Juliet's house for a game of tag, he did not show up. Juliet waited for two hours. Then she went out to look for him.

She found him at his house having a snack with August, the new cat on the block.

Juliet was very mad.
She poured a pitcher of tomato juice all over Rollo.

"Why did you do that, Juliet?" asked Rollo.
"I just felt like it," said Juliet. "I just had a terrible urge to dump tomato juice on you."

"It must be the same urge I have to dump this carton of buttermilk all over you," said Rollo.
And he poured a carton of buttermilk on Juliet.

"I hate buttermilk and I hate you!" cried Juliet.
"I hate you too!" yelled Rollo.

Juliet ran home and sat in her bathtub. "That's the end of true blue," she said. "I'll never speak to Rollo again."

Rollo sat in his bathtub. "Forever is all over," he said as he watched his bath water turn pink. "I'll never speak to Juliet again."

The next day Juliet and Rollo saw each other at the grocery store.

"I guess he's storing up buttermilk," thought Juliet.

"I bet she's buying out the entire stock of tomato juice," thought Rollo.

Juliet and Rollo were careful not to speak to each other.

"Not a word will I say to that ill-tempered Juliet," thought Rollo.

"Notice that I'm saying nothing to you," said Juliet as she passed by Rollo.

"I noticed," said Rollo. "I'm talking to myself when I say I noticed. I am not talking to you, Juliet."

Juliet shook a can of tomato juice at Rollo, and she left the store.

Rollo walked home with his packages. "Being mad at Juliet is the very best thing that ever happened to me," he thought. "It's better than winning at tag or being able to sing high C. It's better than being clever or handsome or even having a good friend."

Juliet walked home. She thought, "I am furious at Rollo, and fury feels wonderful. It has a zing and a ring to it, like dozens of bells clanging at the same time."

When Juliet got home she flung fifteen pairs of socks at the wall, she hit her stuffed fish with a baseball bat and she ripped up her SMILE poster.

"Wonderful, it feels wonderful," she said, gritting her teeth.

Meanwhile Rollo relaxed at home and drank a glass of buttermilk. "Here's to total hatred," he said. "Here's to the feeling that I want to pour oceans and oceans of buttermilk over someone named Juliet Cat."

For two entire weeks Rollo and Juliet enjoyed hating each other. But one day Rollo woke up and didn't quite feel so mad at Juliet. "What's a little tomato juice compared to a beautiful friendship?" he thought.

Juliet noticed that she was hardly ever throwing socks or hitting her stuffed fish or ripping posters. "I guess I'm not mad anymore," she thought. "But how can I tell Rollo? We're not even talking."

Juliet went to her telephone. She called Rollo. She said, "Hello," and hung up.

"Well, well, well," thought Rollo. "One word from Juliet. It's a start."

Rollo called Juliet. "Hello back," he said, and then he hung up.

Rollo kept thinking about Juliet's hello. "I could hear the friendship oozing through her voice."

Rollo ran over to Juliet's house and stood under her window. "Juliet, Juliet," he called. "I came over here because I could hear friendship oozing through your voice."

Juliet leaned out her window.

Rollo went on. "I know you are sorry that you dumped one full quart of tomato juice on me. I know that you have been sitting around your house thinking about all of my wonderful qualities and missing each and every one of them."

"What?" screamed Juliet.

Rollo went on. "I know that you want to say I'M SORRY, I'M SORRY, I'M SORRY. Well, here I am, and you can say it to me."

"What? <u>You're</u> the one who should be sorry," screamed Juliet again. "I'm GLAD I dumped tomato juice on you. I'm glad, glad, glad."

And Juliet poured a pitcher of limeade all over Rollo.

"That's no way to say I'm sorry," shouted Rollo, and he ran home and took a shower.

"Something went wrong," thought Rollo. "Otherwise I wouldn't be all wet and green." Rollo blow-dried his fur. "I know Juliet wants to talk to me. That's why she said hello."

Meanwhile, Juliet washed and dried her pitcher, and thought, "Something went wrong. I know that Rollo wants to talk to me. That's why he said hello back."

Rollo and Juliet decided to speak to each other. When they passed on the street, Juliet would say, "Good-bye forever."

And Rollo would answer, "Good-bye forever back."

As time went on, their conversations got longer. "I would like to tell you all the ways I don't like you," Juliet said one day.

"Okay," said Rollo. "Come to my house and sit on my sofa and tell me."

"All right," said Juliet.

Rollo and Juliet went to Rollo's house.

"Well," said Juliet, "I don't like you when you pour things on me and when you try to make up and you don't."

"That's how I feel about you," said Rollo.

Rollo and Juliet sat and looked at each other for a long time.

Then Rollo said, "I remember something I want to remember."

"So do I," said Juliet. "I remember the ways I like you."

"Yes," said Rollo. "Through sad times, good times, rain, sleet, crackling thunder and prickly heat."

"Maybe we should make up," said Juliet.

"Forever," said Rollo.

"At least," said Juliet.

And so Rollo and Juliet once again became friends forever. So far they have had only thirty-four fights, but they've made up every time.